The QUOKKAS, the SNAILS, and the LAND of HAPPINESS

ERIC GEIGER & EVIE GEIGER

ILLUSTRATIONS BY
PABLO PINO

B&H
kids
Nashville TN

DEDICATIONS

Eric—I am thankful for the teachers who invest in children and teenagers and help them discover their gifts and passions. Thank you, Ms. Landry, for helping me love stories and literature. You made me a better storyteller for my kids and those I serve.

Evie—I am thankful for my teachers, who encourage me to be creative and try new things. Thank you, Mrs. Lang, for helping me love to write. I will never forget my second-grade year with you!

Dewey Decimal Classification: C248.82
Subject Heading: HAPPINESS / JOY AND SORROW / CHRISTIAN LIFE

All Scripture quotations are taken from the Christian Standard Bible®, copyright © 2017 by Holman Bible Publishers. Used by permission. Christian Standard Bible® and CSB® are federally registered trademarks of Holman Bible Publishers.

Printed in November 2020 in ShenZhen, Guangdong, China
1 2 3 4 5 6 • 24 23 22 21 20

PART 1

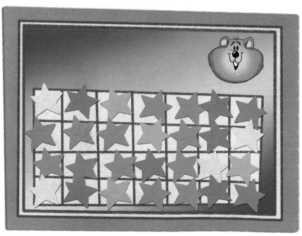

This is a story about two families. Both families had two kids who brushed their teeth and went to school every morning. Both families had one child who *always* had to be reminded to brush his teeth, which sometimes made both families late for school. Both moms made pancakes for breakfast. Both dads misplaced their keys. Both families had lots of socks but struggled to find ones that matched.

It may sound like the families were very similar. But if you knew them, you would know they were different from one another. Very different.

The first family, the Quokkas, lived in the Land of Happiness. It was joyful, even when days were tough. Their lives were not perfect, but they were filled with hope and peace. Their home overflowed with smiles and hugs and somersaults and jumps. They loved playing and eating and laughing together. They loved life.

The Quokka family was so grateful to be living in the Land of Happiness. They had not always lived there, but that's a much longer story.

A few miles away was the Land of
Sadness, where the Snail family lived. Well,
some might call what they did "living," but
really they were only breathing and slowly
moving through life. Actually, it was more
like crawling through life. Their days were
long and sad. Very sad.

You may be wondering, *Why didn't the Snails leave the Land of Sadness?* The short answer is that they didn't know life could be lived any other way. In fact, most people in that land didn't even know the name of the place where they lived. They just kept going through the motions, crawling through life one day at a time.

As different as the two families were, and although they lived in two different lands, each family had the same tradition: they began the day with sticker charts and a family motto. But their mornings did not feel the same . . .

In the Land of Sadness, the Snails recited their motto:

*Work hard every single day
to fill your chart up all the way.*

"Say it louder!" they would sluggishly shout. And every day the Snail children—Sam and Suzy—would say even louder, "WORK HARD every single day to FILL YOUR CHART up all the way."

Both Snail children had a chart, and every time Sam helped his mom or dad or Suzy was kind to a neighbor, the kids could put a sticker on the chart. And when the chart was full, they could go to the store and buy a snailish toy. Sounds great, doesn't it? Well, it wasn't.

11

Sam and Suzy thought the next sticker or the next toy would bring happiness, but it never did. Under their beds were toys they never played with, toys that always sounded like they would be more fun than they really were.

Obeying their parents, being kind, or sharing with friends wasn't satisfying at all when it was done only for a sticker. And no matter what, Sam and Suzy always needed *more* stickers because as soon as one chart was filled there was always another chart waiting. Life was sad and tiring. Really, really tiring. Snailish, actually.

The Snail kids had hearts filled with . . .
Actually, their hearts weren't filled at all.
Their hearts felt empty and got smaller and
smaller each day. They couldn't really see it
happening, but over time they knew.

Each day when the Quokka children—
Kenton and Kailey—woke up in the Land
of Happiness, they bounced into the kitchen
for breakfast and saw their sticker charts
completely filled. Then they shared their
family motto:

Be grateful and enjoy your day.
Your chart is filled in every way!

The kids danced around the kitchen
because their charts were always full. They
never took a sticker off or added a sticker.

Life was not exhausting for the Quokka family. Kenton and Kailey did not have to worry about doing enough good things or saying enough right things to earn a sticker. They had chores (of course), and they were expected to be kind to one another (of course)—but not to fill their charts. They wanted to be helpful and kind *because* their charts were already filled!

The Quokka kids had only a few toys under their beds, yet they were happy. They were joyful because they were thankful . . . thankful that their sticker charts were always filled. They did not have to live for stickers! They were eager to help their parents and share with friends because they were grateful for what they had been given.

Kenton and Kailey Quokka had hearts filled with joy. Their hearts felt full, and as crazy as it sounds, their hearts got bigger and bigger each day. They could not really see it happening, but over time they knew.

But this story is not just about two very different families from two different lands with two very different sticker charts. This is really a story about a rare day when two young snails and two young quokkas found themselves at the same strawberry patch.

PART 2

Between the Land of Happiness and the Land of Sadness stretched a giant field of strawberries. Kenton and Kailey Quokka loved that field. They were always thankful to be able to hop through the rows and pick amazing strawberries. They giggled as the juice spilled from the huge, red berries onto their shirts, and then they licked the strawberry juice that made their fingers red and yummy.

So one Tuesday afternoon when
Mama Quokka suggested the family have
strawberry shortcake for dessert, Kailey and
Kenton squealed with joy. "We get to go to
the field!" They scurried out with a hop in
their steps. The field was a gift, a gift they
enjoyed.

As the Quokka kids headed down the path, Kailey slowed her hop a bit so Kenton could keep up. "How are you feeling today? How are your legs?" she asked.

"I've had better days, but I'm thinking about those strawberries right now!" said her brother. When Kenton was born, the doctors said his legs didn't work as they should. He had trouble keeping up with other kids, but his parents told him his legs were a gift that would help him slow down and enjoy all the sights and sounds around him.

Today Kenton was busy talking about all he saw, which was not unusual. He was always outgoing and lots of fun. When he realized he was doing most of the talking, he asked his sister about her day. "How was your big test?"

"I think I did well," Kailey said. "The teacher gave me extra time, which was great."

As Kenton continued to chat, Kailey mainly listened. She was kind and sweet, but she liked thinking about her words before saying them. She had a learning disability, so she talked more slowly than her mind worked. It was hard for her to speak with confidence in front of people. Although she always felt comfortable with Kenton, she was still happy to let him do most of the talking while she enjoyed their walk—the green grass, the way the sky looked, the feeling of the sun on the back of her neck, and the breeze hitting her quokka face.

As you can see, life was sometimes hard for the Quokkas. The Land of Happiness was not perfect, but it was still filled with joy and peace. And it was filled with hope, hope that one day all things would be perfect.

That same Tuesday afternoon, Mama Snail was also thinking about strawberries. But Sam and Suzy Snail did not like the strawberry field. Instead of enjoying the berries, they complained about the mud or the bugs or the tall, itchy grass. And they really did not like having to take a bath after getting the yucky, sticky strawberry juice on their snaily hands.

When Mama Snail asked Sam and Suzy to gather berries for that night's strawberry pie, she reminded them, "If you fetch strawberries, you get a sticker to add to your charts."

Sam grumbled, "It's really hot outside!" Suzy whined, "It's an awful lot of walking for just one sticker. We should get two stickers!"

Mama Snail gave them a look and said, "We will see when you get back." So off they went to the field with their heads down, only going for the stickers. The field was a chore, a chore they did not enjoy.

Suzy and Sam left the Snail house with one goal in mind: get the strawberries to get the stickers. "Work hard every single day to fill your chart up all the way," they said in their not-so-happy voices.

Suzy was the oldest. She was confident
and talented. People really liked her, but
she didn't feel well liked, at least not most
of the time. She worked so hard at so
many things: volleyball, school, piano, and
painting. And of course, she did all these
things to get stickers for her sticker chart.

But she worried too. Was she good enough at everything? Would she get better? It felt as if she would never be able to rest.

"Let's pick those berries as fast as we can," she said to Sam. "I still have to practice piano, *and* I have homework! At least I finished my painting this morning."

"Please. Stop. Bragging. I already know how awesome you are. Let's just get to the field!" blurted out Sam.

It was a lot for Sam to say. He was the quiet Snail kid, at least compared to Suzy. And he was used to being compared to his sister: *"Oh, you're Suzy's brother. Do you paint as well as she does? Are you good at volleyball like your sister? Are you smart like Suzy?"*

Sam had not admitted this to anyone, but he had given up. He thought he would never be good enough to earn respect and attention from others, and his sticker chart reminded him of this every day. He imagined that when he was older, he would leave this land and go somewhere far, far away. There had to be some other way to live in some other land, and he wanted to find it. For now, picking these ridiculous strawberries was the price he had to pay for living in the Snail home and eating Snail strawberry pie so he could sleep in his Snail bed and dream of a new place.

Suzy and Sam Snail raced as fast as they could to a patch of strawberries in the middle of the field. Well, in their minds, they were going fast. But in reality, they weren't going fast at all. They were snails, after all.

Everyone in the Land of Sadness always felt like they were moving fast. They worked hard, just like the Snail family. But life in the Land of Sadness always felt faster and more productive than it really was. Sam thought it was all "meaningless, just meaningless."

So the Quokka kids and the Snail kids felt very differently about the strawberry field. But they were now going to find themselves sharing the patch for the very first time. And that day would change everything.

PART 3

Hurry up. Let's fill this basket and head back home!" Suzy Snail shouted to Sam Snail, who held the basket as Suzy dropped a berry in without even looking at it.

I can't hold the basket any faster, he thought, but he decided not to say so because he was glad his sister was doing all the picking.

Not far away, Kenton Quokka was too busy enjoying the strawberry patch to notice that two other kids were picking from it. He watched the red of the berries change as clouds passed in front of the sun, and he enjoyed smelling the berries' sweetness. And tasting it too. For every strawberry he placed in the basket, he put another in his mouth.

As she happily filled her basket, Kailey was the first to see the Snail siblings a few rows away. Just then Suzy looked up, and her snail eyes met Kailey's quokka eyes for the first time. There they were, in the middle of a strawberry patch, picking berries for different reasons, staring at one another.

Kailey waved shyly. Suzy Snail spoke first, as she always did. "Hi, I'm Suzy, and this is my brother, Sam."

Kenton Quokka, in the middle of a juicy berry bite, answered, "Hi! We're Kenton and Kailey Quokka. Aren't these strawberries awesome? Look how big and juicy they are!"

Sam Snail started to roll his eyes, but Suzy gave him a quick glance that told him

to behave. "I'm sure the strawberries are amazing," she said, "but we're just doing our chores so we can get home and get our stickers for our charts."

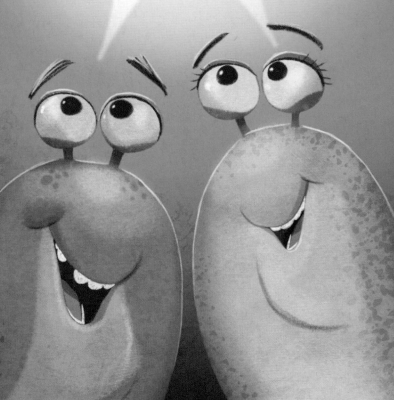

Suzy was trying to rush the conversation, and those words had just slipped out of her mouth. She realized how odd sticker charts might sound to the Quokkas. She thought to herself, *What if they don't have sticker charts? Does it sound crazy that I'm picking strawberries just to get a sticker?*

But then Kenton blurted, "We have sticker charts too, but ours are always full! We don't have to earn stickers."

Sam could not believe what he had just heard—*he didn't have to earn stickers?* As his sister continued to talk to the Quokkas, his mind drifted to thinking about that sort of life. He had always hoped for something different than constantly working to fill a chart, only to have to fill another, and then another. Was there truly a place where that was possible?

He looked down at a strawberry in his basket. He imagined it would taste so much better if he could just enjoy it and not feel the pressure to use it to get a sticker. What would life be like without "work hard every single day to fill your chart up all the way" ringing in his ears all the time? He was tired of feeling like he had to *do* things to be someone, like he had to work hard to be loved and noticed. And he was tired of saying their motto louder and louder. He felt he could never say it as loud as he should.

Meanwhile, as Kailey listened to Suzy describe how the snails had to work and work to fill their sticker charts and earn approval, she was reminded why she loved the Land of Happiness. Their motto flashed

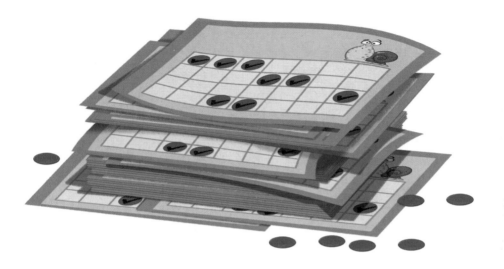

in her mind: "Be grateful and enjoy your day; your chart is filled in every way!" Her problems seemed to fade as her heart grew more and more thankful. She thought about what life must feel like for the Snails, who lived in a land where you had to earn your way each day and work hard to feel accepted and loved.

Almost at the exact same moment, Kailey Quokka and Sam Snail blurted, "What is life like on the other side?" At that moment, all four kids realized they lived not just on other sides of the field but in completely different lands.

The next few seconds of silence felt a lot longer. Kenton Quokka was the first to speak (of course). He said, "We've loved the Land of Happiness ever since we moved there."

Kailey Quokka suddenly had so much to say. "Life is not perfect," she began, "but the Creator is. He started the Land of Happiness, and because of Him our sticker charts are always full! We used to live for stickers, but not anymore. Now we do things *because* we have all the stickers!

We used to worry about impressing our parents and our teachers and our coaches and our friends' parents and everyone else. Life was not happy at all. Nowadays, we still mess up, *a lot*, but we don't live to prove ourselves. We still have chores and homework, and we still work hard. But we don't have to earn love. We already *are* loved."

Suzy Snail had never heard anything like this. With excitement she asked, "So if I fill my sticker chart in the Land of Happiness, I will never have to fill it again?"

"No, it's even better than that!" Kenton Quokka almost shouted. "You never have to fill your chart at all. You believe in the Creator, and He fills your chart for you! All you do is receive! That is really what the Land of Happiness is all about."

Sam Snail had been listening and taking this all in. He had imagined such a land, and now he knew it was real. He raised his hand (that was the only way he could get a word in), and he yelled the one thing he had been thinking: "I am tired of doing everything to achieve stickers. I want to receive them!"

Suzy Snail saw the pain and the excitement in her brother, whom she loved so much. She understood the pressure he always felt, and she too was tired of living to earn stickers, of constantly trying to achieve more and more. She said, "When we get home, Sam and I are going to talk to our parents about this new land. Maybe we can move there! You two have been so kind to us. And not even for stickers!"

They all smiled.

Kailey said, "How about we meet here every Tuesday an hour before the sun goes down? We can answer any questions you have about the land we live in."

The Snail siblings both nodded, and Suzy said, "Absolutely. That would be great."

With excitement and strawberry stains on his face, Kenton pumped his fists and hollered, "Yay! We would love to help! And I can also help you eat your strawberries if your basket gets too full."

"I don't think you need any more strawberries," Kailey said. And they all laughed.

Kailey and Kenton Quokka couldn't stop smiling as they turned toward home. Sure, they had their problems, but their sticker charts had been filled by their Creator. The strawberries in their baskets were gifts they could enjoy, not merely ways to earn a sticker or two. Life was not perfect, but it was free and full.

As Suzy and Sam Snail headed back across the field, the clouds didn't seem quite as gloomy overhead. They couldn't stop thinking about the big conversation they were going to have with their parents

about where and how to live. Now that Suzy and Sam knew about the Land of Happiness and the Creator, they had a sense that everything was going to change for the better.

Behind the Story

The Sticker Chart—There are two ways to live, *for* approval or *from* approval. Many people live to earn their happiness or to get approval from God. In fact, that is what religion is: people's attempt to earn God. Others live *from* approval, like the Quokkas. The Quokkas obey, share, and show love not to earn God's approval but because God has already approved and accepted them. Because of Jesus' sacrifice on the cross, He gives all who believe in Him His forgiveness and His righteousness. Those who believe in Him stand right before God with nothing to prove!

The Land of Happiness—The Land of Happiness represents the kingdom of God, living life under King Jesus' reign. In Jesus' famous sermon in Matthew 5, He described the blessed or happy life in His kingdom. Although life in His kingdom is not yet perfect, it will be one day!

The Quokkas—Quokkas are known as the world's happiest animals. Although Kenton and Kailey have challenges in their lives, they are ultimately happy because of the King and the kingdom in which they live.

The Land of Sadness—The wisdom writer described "life under the sun" as striving for accomplishments, possessions, and happiness but realizing everything is meaningless (Ecclesiastes 1:2–3). Life is meaningless if you stay out of God's kingdom—out of the Land of Happiness.

The Snails—The Snails are slow and look rather sad. Life "under the sun" can sometimes feel fast and productive, but little is accomplished in the end.

The Creator—Jesus created the world, and He is its King. He is unlike all other kings because He gives forgiveness and grace to those who trust Him. Instead of demanding that we achieve, He asks that we simply believe in Him to receive His goodness.

The Good News About the Sticker Chart

Every kid and every parent and every person has the same decision, the same choice. Do you live to earn, or do you live because Jesus has earned life for you? Do you constantly feel pressure to *do*, or do you enjoy because it has already been *done*?

Do you "work hard every single day to fill your chart up all the way"? Or are you "grateful and enjoy your day" because your chart is filled in every way?

Now to the one who works, pay is not credited as a gift, but as something owed. But to the one who does not work, but believes on him who justifies the ungodly, his faith is credited for righteousness. Just as David also speaks of the blessing of the person to whom God credits righteousness apart from works:
Blessed are those whose lawless acts are forgiven and whose sins are covered. Blessed is the person the Lord will never charge with sin.

—Romans 4:4–8

There are basically two ways to live. We can work and work and work, trying to fill our sticker charts and make ourselves happy with what we achieve. Or we can trust God to make us happy and receive His love and forgiveness.

We can approach God in two ways. We can work hard trying to make ourselves right with God, or we can stop working and trust the work Jesus has already done for us. If we work to fill our sticker charts, we are never satisfied and the sticker chart will never be filled because we all fall short of God's perfect standard. If we stop trusting our own work and trust Jesus and His finished work for us on the cross—where He died to take away our sins and give us His perfection—He fills in all the stickers!

Eric Geiger serves as the senior pastor of Mariners Church in Orange County, California. He received his doctorate in leadership and church ministry from Southern Seminary. Eric has authored or co-authored several books, including the best-selling church leadership book *Simple Church*. He is married to Kaye, and they have two daughters: Eden and Evie. During his free time, Eric enjoys dating his wife, taking his daughters to the beach, and mountain biking. Evie is, by far, his favorite co-author.

Evie Geiger is an eleven-year-old who loves Jesus, loves people, and believes life should be fun and creative. Evie is always working on some creative project to bring people together, make them smile, and point them to the One who gives us ultimate joy. This is her first book, and she loved working on it with her dad. The "sticker chart" example is how Eric and Evie have often talked about the two different approaches to life. She is thankful her chart is completely filled.